S0-AKH-725

WITHDRAWN
Damaged, Obsolete, or Surplus
Jackson County Library Services

THIS CANDLEWICK BOOK BELONGS TO:

_____

_____

_____

Golden Goose as told by Jacob Grimm and Wilhelm Grimm, Tom Thumb as told by Richard Johnson, The Golden Bird as told by Jacob Grimm and Wilhelm Grimm, Snow-White and Rose-Red as told by Jacob
by Bram Stoker ∽ THE ROPE ∽ Rapunzel as told by Jacob Grimm and Wilhelm Grimm ∽ THE CLOUDS ∽ Suo Gân as adapted by Robert Bryan, Twinkle, Twinkle, Little Star by Jane Taylor, Hush-a-Bye Baby as ad
ay Alcott, The Three Musketeers by Alexandre Dumas, The Tale of Peter Rabbit by Beatrix Potter, Alice's Adventures in Wonderland by Lewis Carroll, Great Expectations by Charles Dickens, Adventures of Huckleberry
Malory and Sir James Knowles and Rip Van Winkle by Washington Irving ∽ THE SEA ∽ The Voyages of Doctor Dolittle by Hugh Lofting, The Swiss Family Robinson by Johann David Wyss, Robinson Crusoe by Danie
n Crusoe by Daniel Defoe, The Swiss Family Robinson by Johann David Wyss, The Adventures of Pinocchio by Carlo Collodi and Twenty Thousand Leagues Under the Sea by Jules Verne ∽ THE HOLE ∽ Alice's Adv
mm and Wilhelm Grimm, Hansel & Gretel as told by Jacob Grimm and Wilhelm Grimm, The Golden Goose as told by Jacob Grimm and Wilhelm Grimm, Tom Thumb as told by Richard Johnson, The Golden Bird as told
nd of Sleepy Hollow by Washington Irving, Frankenstein by Mary Shelley and Dracula by Bram Stoker ∽ THE ROPE ∽ Rapunzel as told by Jacob Grimm and Wilhelm Grimm ∽ THE CLOUDS ∽ Suo Gân as adapted
nk Baum, The Wind in the Willows by Kenneth Grahame, Little Women by Louisa May Alcott, The Three Musketeers by Alexandre Dumas, The Tale of Peter Rabbit by Beatrix Potter, Alice's Adventures in Wonderland
auty by Anna Sewell, The Legends of King Arthur and His Knights by Sir Thomas Malory and Sir James Knowles and Rip Van Winkle by Washington Irving ∽ THE SEA ∽ The Voyages of Doctor Dolittle by Hugh Lof
e Sea by Jules Verne ∽ THE WAVE ∽ Gulliver's Travels by Jonathan Swift, Robinson Crusoe by Daniel Defoe, The Swiss Family Robinson by Johann David Wyss, The Adventures of Pinocchio by Carlo Collodi and Tw
ed by Robert Louis Stevenson ∽ THE FOREST ∽ Little Red-Cap as told by Jacob Grimm and Wilhelm Grimm, Hansel & Gretel as told by Jacob Grimm and Wilhelm Grimm, The Golden Goose as told by Jacob Grimm ar
unzel as told by Jacob Grimm and Wilhelm Grimm ∽ THE MONSTER ∽ The Legend of Sleepy Hollow by Washington Irving, Frankenstein by Mary Shelley and Dracula by Bram Stoker ∽ THE ROPE ∽ Rapunzel as t
he Moon by Jules Verne ∽ THE WORLD ∽ The Wonderful Wizard of Oz by L. Frank Baum, The Wind in the Willows by Kenneth Grahame, Little Women by Louisa May Alcott, The Three Musketeers by Alexandre D
Melville, The Secret Garden by Frances Hodgson Burnett, Heidi by Johanna Spyri, Black Beauty by Anna Sewell, The Legends of King Arthur and His Knights by Sir Thomas Malory and Sir James Knowles and Rip Van W
venson, Gulliver's Travels by Jonathan Swift and Twenty Thousand Leagues Under the Sea by Jules Verne ∽ THE WAVE ∽ Gulliver's Travels by Jonathan Swift, Robinson Crusoe by Daniel Defoe, The Swiss Family Ro
y J.M. Barrie ∽ THE CAVE ∽ Treasure Island by Robert Louis Stevenson and Kidnapped by Robert Louis Stevenson ∽ THE FOREST ∽ Little Red-Cap as told by Jacob Grimm and Wilhelm Grimm, Hansel & Gretel as
nd Wilhelm Grimm, Beauty and the Beast by Jeanne-Marie Leprince de Beaumont and Rapunzel as told by Jacob Grimm and Wilhelm Grimm ∽ THE MONSTER ∽ The Legend of Sleepy Hollow by Washington Irving, F
y John Newbery and Brahms' Lullaby by Johannes Brahms ∽ THE MOON ∽ Around the Moon by Jules Verne ∽ THE WORLD ∽ The Wonderful Wizard of Oz by L. Frank Baum, The Wind in the Willows by Kenne
n by Mark Twain, A Christmas Carol by Charles Dickens, Moby-Dick by Herman Melville, The Secret Garden by Frances Hodgson Burnett, Heidi by Johanna Spyri, Black Beauty by Anna Sewell, The Legends of King A
efoe, The Count of Monte Cristo by Alexandre Dumas, Kidnapped by Robert Louis Stevenson, Gulliver's Travels by Jonathan Swift and Twenty Thousand Leagues Under the Sea by Jules Verne ∽ THE WAVE ∽ Gullive
res in Wonderland by Lewis Carroll ∽ THE MOUNTAINS ∽ Peter Pan and Wendy by J.M. Barrie ∽ THE CAVE ∽ Treasure Island by Robert Louis Stevenson and Kidnapped by Robert Louis Stevenson ∽ THE FORES
cob Grimm and Wilhelm Grimm, Snow-White and Rose-Red as told by Jacob Grimm and Wilhelm Grimm, Beauty and the Beast by Jeanne-Marie Leprince de Beaumont and Rapunzel as told by Jacob Grimm and Wilhelm
y Robert Bryan, Twinkle, Twinkle, Little Star by Jane Taylor, Hush-a-Bye Baby as adapted by John Newbery and Brahms' Lullaby by Johannes Brahms ∽ THE MOON ∽ Around the Moon by Jules Verne ∽ THE WORL
and by Lewis Carroll, Great Expectations by Charles Dickens, Adventures of Huckleberry Finn by Mark Twain, A Christmas Carol by Charles Dickens, Moby-Dick by Herman Melville, The Secret Garden by Frances Ho
fting, The Swiss Family Robinson by Johann David Wyss, Robinson Crusoe by Daniel Defoe, The Count of Monte Cristo by Alexandre Dumas, Kidnapped by Robert Louis Stevenson, Gulliver's Travels by Jonathan Swift a
Thousand Leagues Under the Sea by Jules Verne ∽ THE HOLE ∽ Alice's Adventures in Wonderland by Lewis Carroll ∽ THE MOUNTAINS ∽ Peter Pan and Wendy by J.M. Barrie ∽ THE CAVE ∽ Treasure Island
elm Grimm, Tom Thumb as told by Richard Johnson, The Golden Bird as told by Jacob Grimm and Wilhelm Grimm, Snow-White and Rose-Red as told by Jacob Grimm and Wilhelm Grimm, Beauty and the Beast by Jean
Jacob Grimm and Wilhelm Grimm ∽ THE CLOUDS ∽ Suo Gân as adapted by Robert Bryan, Twinkle, Twinkle, Little Star by Jane Taylor, Hush-a-Bye Baby as adapted by John Newbery and Brahms' Lullaby by Johanne
The Tale of Peter Rabbit by Beatrix Potter, Alice's Adventures in Wonderland by Lewis Carroll, Great Expectations by Charles Dickens, Adventures of Huckleberry Finn by Mark Twain, A Christmas Carol by Charles D
ngton Irving ∽ THE SEA ∽ The Voyages of Doctor Dolittle by Hugh Lofting, The Swiss Family Robinson by Johann David Wyss, Robinson Crusoe by Daniel Defoe, The Count of Monte Cristo by Alexandre Dumas, K
David Wyss, The Adventures of Pinocchio by Carlo Collodi and Twenty Thousand Leagues Under the Sea by Jules Verne ∽ THE HOLE ∽ Alice's Adventures in Wonderland by Lewis Carroll ∽ THE MOUNTAINS ∽
nd Wilhelm Grimm, The Golden Goose as told by Jacob Grimm and Wilhelm Grimm, Tom Thumb as told by Richard Johnson, The Golden Bird as told by Jacob Grimm and Wilhelm Grimm, Snow-White and Rose-Red as
lley and Dracula by Bram Stoker ∽ THE ROPE ∽ Rapunzel as told by Jacob Grimm and Wilhelm Grimm ∽ THE CLOUDS ∽ Suo Gân as adapted by Robert Bryan, Twinkle, Twinkle, Little Star by Jane Taylor, Hush-a-
omen by Louisa May Alcott, The Three Musketeers by Alexandre Dumas, The Tale of Peter Rabbit by Beatrix Potter, Alice's Adventures in Wonderland by Lewis Carroll, Great Expectations by Charles Dickens, Adventure
by Sir Thomas Malory and Sir James Knowles and Rip Van Winkle by Washington Irving ∽ THE SEA ∽ The Voyages of Doctor Dolittle by Hugh Lofting, The Swiss Family Robinson by Johann David Wyss, Robinson C
Swift, Robinson Crusoe by Daniel Defoe, The Swiss Family Robinson by Johann David Wyss, The Adventures of Pinocchio by Carlo Collodi and Twenty Thousand Leagues Under the Sea by Jules Verne ∽ THE HOLE
as told by Jacob Grimm and Wilhelm Grimm, Hansel & Gretel as told by Jacob Grimm and Wilhelm Grimm, The Golden Goose as told by Jacob Grimm and Wilhelm Grimm, Tom Thumb as told by Richard Johnson, The G
NSTER ∽ The Legend of Sleepy Hollow by Washington Irving, Frankenstein by Mary Shelley and Dracula by Bram Stoker ∽ THE ROPE ∽ Rapunzel as told by Jacob Grimm and Wilhelm Grimm ∽ THE CLOUDS
ful Wizard of Oz by L. Frank Baum, The Wind in the Willows by Kenneth Grahame, Little Women by Louisa May Alcott, The Three Musketeers by Alexandre Dumas, The Tale of Peter Rabbit by Beatrix Potter, Alice's A
Johanna Spyri, Black Beauty by Anna Sewell, The Legends of King Arthur and His Knights by Sir Thomas Malory and Sir James Knowles and Rip Van Winkle by Washington Irving ∽ THE SEA ∽ The Voyages of Doc
d Leagues Under the Sea by Jules Verne ∽ THE WAVE ∽ Gulliver's Travels by Jonathan Swift, Robinson Crusoe by Daniel Defoe, The Swiss Family Robinson by Johann David Wyss, The Adventures of Pinocchio by C
venson and Kidnapped by Robert Louis Stevenson ∽ THE FOREST ∽ Little Red-Cap as told by Jacob Grimm and Wilhelm Grimm, Hansel & Gretel as told by Jacob Grimm and Wilhelm Grimm, The Golden Goose as to
de Beaumont and Rapunzel as told by Jacob Grimm and Wilhelm Grimm ∽ THE MONSTER ∽ The Legend of Sleepy Hollow by Washington Irving, Frankenstein by Mary Shelley and Dracula by Bram Stoker ∽ THE R
MOON ∽ Around the Moon by Jules Verne ∽ THE WORLD ∽ The Wonderful Wizard of Oz by L. Frank Baum, The Wind in the Willows by Kenneth Grahame, Little Women by Louisa May Alcott, The Three Muske
ick by Herman Melville, The Secret Garden by Frances Hodgson Burnett, Heidi by Johanna Spyri, Black Beauty by Anna Sewell, The Legends of King Arthur and His Knights by Sir Thomas Malory and Sir James Knowles
ed by Robert Louis Stevenson, Gulliver's Travels by Jonathan Swift and Twenty Thousand Leagues Under the Sea by Jules Verne ∽ THE WAVE ∽ Gulliver's Travels by Jonathan Swift, Robinson Crusoe by Daniel Defoe,
Pan and Wendy by J.M. Barrie ∽ THE CAVE ∽ Treasure Island by Robert Louis Stevenson and Kidnapped by Robert Louis Stevenson ∽ THE FOREST ∽ Little Red-Cap as told by Jacob Grimm and Wilhelm Grimm, H
Jacob Grimm and Wilhelm Grimm, Beauty and the Beast by Jeanne-Marie Leprince de Beaumont and Rapunzel as told by Jacob Grimm and Wilhelm Grimm ∽ THE MONSTER ∽ The Legend of Sleepy Hollow by Wash
Bye Baby as adapted by John Newbery and Brahms' Lullaby by Johannes Brahms ∽ THE MOON ∽ Around the Moon by Jules Verne ∽ THE WORLD ∽ The Wonderful Wizard of Oz by L. Frank Baum, The Wind in
res of Huckleberry Finn by Mark Twain, A Christmas Carol by Charles Dickens, Moby-Dick by Herman Melville, The Secret Garden by Frances Hodgson Burnett, Heidi by Johanna Spyri, Black Beauty by Anna Sewell, T
n Crusoe by Daniel Defoe, The Count of Monte Cristo by Alexandre Dumas, Kidnapped by Robert Louis Stevenson, Gulliver's Travels by Jonathan Swift and Twenty Thousand Leagues Under the Sea by Jules Verne ∽ T
Alice's Adventures in Wonderland by Lewis Carroll ∽ THE MOUNTAINS ∽ Peter Pan and Wendy by J.M. Barrie ∽ THE CAVE ∽ Treasure Island by Robert Louis Stevenson and Kidnapped by Robert Louis Stevenso
Bird as told by Jacob Grimm and Wilhelm Grimm, Snow-White and Rose-Red as told by Jacob Grimm and Wilhelm Grimm, Beauty and the Beast by Jeanne-Marie Leprince de Beaumont and Rapunzel as told by Jacob Grin
as adapted by Robert Bryan, Twinkle, Twinkle, Little Star by Jane Taylor, Hush-a-Bye Baby as adapted by John Newbery and Brahms' Lullaby by Johannes Brahms ∽ THE MOON ∽ Around the Moon by Jules Verne
res in Wonderland by Lewis Carroll, Great Expectations by Charles Dickens, Adventures of Huckleberry Finn by Mark Twain, A Christmas Carol by Charles Dickens, Moby-Dick by Herman Melville, The Secret Garde
Dolittle by Hugh Lofting, The Swiss Family Robinson by Johann David Wyss, Robinson Crusoe by Daniel Defoe, The Count of Monte Cristo by Alexandre Dumas, Kidnapped by Robert Louis Stevenson, Gulliver's Travel
Collodi and Twenty Thousand Leagues Under the Sea by Jules Verne ∽ THE HOLE ∽ Alice's Adventures in Wonderland by Lewis Carroll ∽ THE MOUNTAINS ∽ Peter Pan and Wendy by J.M. Barrie ∽ THE CAV
cob Grimm and Wilhelm Grimm, Tom Thumb as told by Richard Johnson, The Golden Bird as told by Jacob Grimm and Wilhelm Grimm, Snow-White and Rose-Red as told by Jacob Grimm and Wilhelm Grimm, Beauty a
Rapunzel as told by Jacob Grimm and Wilhelm Grimm ∽ THE CLOUDS ∽ Suo Gân as adapted by Robert Bryan, Twinkle, Twinkle, Little Star by Jane Taylor, Hush-a-Bye Baby as adapted by John Newbery and Brahms
ers by Alexandre Dumas, The Tale of Peter Rabbit by Beatrix Potter, Alice's Adventures in Wonderland by Lewis Carroll, Great Expectations by Charles Dickens, Adventures of Huckleberry Finn by Mark Twain, A Chri
and Rip Van Winkle by Washington Irving ∽ THE SEA ∽ The Voyages of Doctor Dolittle by Hugh Lofting, The Swiss Family Robinson by Johann David Wyss, Robinson Crusoe by Daniel Defoe, The Count of Monte
s Family Robinson by Johann David Wyss, The Adventures of Pinocchio by Carlo Collodi and Twenty Thousand Leagues Under the Sea by Jules Verne ∽ THE HOLE ∽ Alice's Adventures in Wonderland by Lewis C

Beauty and the Beast by Jeanne-Marie Leprince de Beaumont and Rapunzel as told by Jacob Grimm and Wilhelm Grimm
y and Brahms' Lullaby by Johannes Brahms ∽ THE MOON ∽ Around the Moon by Jules Verne ∽ THE WORLD ∽ The Wonderful Wizard of Oz by L. Frank Baum, The Wind in the Willows by Kenneth Grahame, L
ain, A Christmas Carol by Charles Dickens, Moby-Dick by Herman Melville, The Secret Garden by Frances Hodgson Burnett, Heidi by Johanna Spyri, Black Beauty by Anna Sewell, The Legends of King Arthur and His
of Monte Cristo by Alexandre Dumas, Kidnapped by Robert Louis Stevenson, Gulliver's Travels by Jonathan Swift and Twenty Thousand Leagues Under the Sea by Jules Verne ∽ THE WAVE ∽ Gulliver's Travels by Jon
land by Lewis Carroll ∽ THE MOUNTAINS ∽ Peter Pan and Wendy by J.M. Barrie ∽ THE CAVE ∽ Treasure Island by Robert Louis Stevenson and Kidnapped by Robert Louis Stevenson ∽ THE FOREST ∽ Little Re
l Wilhelm Grimm, Snow-White and Rose-Red as told by Jacob Grimm and Wilhelm Grimm, Beauty and the Beast by Jeanne-Marie Leprince de Beaumont and Rapunzel as told by Jacob Grimm and Wilhelm Grimm ∽ TH
winkle, Twinkle, Little Star by Jane Taylor, Hush-a-Bye Baby as adapted by John Newbery and Brahms' Lullaby by Johannes Brahms ∽ THE MOON ∽ Around the Moon by Jules Verne ∽ THE WORLD ∽ The Wonde
reat Expectations by Charles Dickens, Adventures of Huckleberry Finn by Mark Twain, A Christmas Carol by Charles Dickens, Moby-Dick by Herman Melville, The Secret Garden by Frances Hodgson Burnett, Heidi b
nily Robinson by Johann David Wyss, Robinson Crusoe by Daniel Defoe, The Count of Monte Cristo by Alexandre Dumas, Kidnapped by Robert Louis Stevenson, Gulliver's Travels by Jonathan Swift and Twenty Thous
agues Under the Sea by Jules Verne ∽ THE HOLE ∽ Alice's Adventures in Wonderland by Lewis Carroll ∽ THE MOUNTAINS ∽ Peter Pan and Wendy by J.M. Barrie ∽ THE CAVE ∽ Treasure Island by Robert Lo
Tom Thumb as told by Richard Johnson, The Golden Bird as told by Jacob Grimm and Wilhelm Grimm, Snow-White and Rose-Red as told by Jacob Grimm and Wilhelm Grimm, Beauty and the Beast by Jeanne-Marie Le
and Wilhelm Grimm ∽ THE CLOUDS ∽ Suo Gân as adapted by Robert Bryan, Twinkle, Twinkle, Little Star by Jane Taylor, Hush-a-Bye Baby as adapted by John Newbery and Brahms' Lullaby by Johannes Brahms ∽ T
Peter Rabbit by Beatrix Potter, Alice's Adventures in Wonderland by Lewis Carroll, Great Expectations by Charles Dickens, Adventures of Huckleberry Finn by Mark Twain, A Christmas Carol by Charles Dickens, Mo
n Irving ∽ THE SEA ∽ The Voyages of Doctor Dolittle by Hugh Lofting, The Swiss Family Robinson by Johann David Wyss, Robinson Crusoe by Daniel Defoe, The Count of Monte Cristo by Alexandre Dumas, Kid
David Wyss, The Adventures of Pinocchio by Carlo Collodi and Twenty Thousand Leagues Under the Sea by Jules Verne ∽ THE HOLE ∽ Alice's Adventures in Wonderland by Lewis Carroll ∽ THE MOUNTAINS ∽
n and Wilhelm Grimm, The Golden Goose as told by Jacob Grimm and Wilhelm Grimm, Tom Thumb as told by Richard Johnson, The Golden Bird as told by Jacob Grimm and Wilhelm Grimm, Snow-White and Rose-Red
ary Shelley and Dracula by Bram Stoker ∽ THE ROPE ∽ Rapunzel as told by Jacob Grimm and Wilhelm Grimm ∽ THE CLOUDS ∽ Suo Gân as adapted by Robert Bryan, Twinkle, Twinkle, Little Star by Jane Taylor, H
Women by Louisa May Alcott, The Three Musketeers by Alexandre Dumas, The Tale of Peter Rabbit by Beatrix Potter, Alice's Adventures in Wonderland by Lewis Carroll, Great Expectations by Charles Dickens, Adven
ghts by Sir Thomas Malory and Sir James Knowles and Rip Van Winkle by Washington Irving ∽ THE SEA ∽ The Voyages of Doctor Dolittle by Hugh Lofting, The Swiss Family Robinson by Johann David Wyss, Robins
an Swift, Robinson Crusoe by Daniel Defoe, The Swiss Family Robinson by Johann David Wyss, The Adventures of Pinocchio by Carlo Collodi and Twenty Thousand Leagues Under the Sea by Jules Verne ∽ THE HC
ap as told by Jacob Grimm and Wilhelm Grimm, Hansel & Gretel as told by Jacob Grimm and Wilhelm Grimm, The Golden Goose as told by Jacob Grimm and Wilhelm Grimm, Tom Thumb as told by Richard Johnson, The
ONSTER ∽ The Legend of Sleepy Hollow by Washington Irving, Frankenstein by Mary Shelley and Dracula by Bram Stoker ∽ THE ROPE ∽ Rapunzel as told by Jacob Grimm and Wilhelm Grimm ∽ THE CLOUDS ∽
ful Wizard of Oz by L. Frank Baum, The Wind in the Willows by Kenneth Grahame, Little Women by Louisa May Alcott, The Three Musketeers by Alexandre Dumas, The Tale of Peter Rabbit by Beatrix Potter, Alice's A
di by Johanna Spyri, Black Beauty by Anna Sewell, The Legends of King Arthur and His Knights by Sir Thomas Malory and Sir James Knowles and Rip Van Winkle by Washington Irving ∽ THE SEA ∽ The Voyages of
and Leagues Under the Sea by Jules Verne ∽ THE WAVE ∽ Gulliver's Travels by Jonathan Swift, Robinson Crusoe by Daniel Defoe, The Swiss Family Robinson by Johann David Wyss, The Adventures of Pinocchio by
venson and Kidnapped by Robert Louis Stevenson ∽ THE FOREST ∽ Little Red-Cap as told by Jacob Grimm and Wilhelm Grimm, Hansel & Gretel as told by Jacob Grimm and Wilhelm Grimm, The Golden Goose as tol
de Beaumont and Rapunzel as told by Jacob Grimm and Wilhelm Grimm ∽ THE MONSTER ∽ The Legend of Sleepy Hollow by Washington Irving, Frankenstein by Mary Shelley and Dracula by Bram Stoker ∽ THE RO
MOON ∽ Around the Moon by Jules Verne ∽ THE WORLD ∽ The Wonderful Wizard of Oz by L. Frank Baum, The Wind in the Willows by Kenneth Grahame, Little Women by Louisa May Alcott, The Three Muske
k by Herman Melville, The Secret Garden by Frances Hodgson Burnett, Heidi by Johanna Spyri, Black Beauty by Anna Sewell, The Legends of King Arthur and His Knights by Sir Thomas Malory and Sir James Knowles an
rt Louis Stevenson, Gulliver's Travels by Jonathan Swift and Twenty Thousand Leagues Under the Sea by Jules Verne ∽ THE WAVE ∽ Gulliver's Travels by Jonathan Swift, Robinson Crusoe by Daniel Defoe, The Swiss
Vendy by J.M. Barrie ∽ THE CAVE ∽ Treasure Island by Robert Louis Stevenson and Kidnapped by Robert Louis Stevenson ∽ THE FOREST ∽ Little Red-Cap as told by Jacob Grimm and Wilhelm Grimm, Hansel & G
m and Wilhelm Grimm, Beauty and the Beast by Jeanne-Marie Leprince de Beaumont and Rapunzel as told by Jacob Grimm and Wilhelm Grimm ∽ THE MONSTER ∽ The Legend of Sleepy Hollow by Washington Irvin
ed by John Newbery and Brahms' Lullaby by Johannes Brahms ∽ THE MOON ∽ Around the Moon by Jules Verne ∽ THE WORLD ∽ The Wonderful Wizard of Oz by L. Frank Baum, The Wind in the Willows by Ke
Finn by Mark Twain, A Christmas Carol by Charles Dickens, Moby-Dick by Herman Melville, The Secret Garden by Frances Hodgson Burnett, Heidi by Johanna Spyri, Black Beauty by Anna Sewell, The Legends of King
efoe, The Count of Monte Cristo by Alexandre Dumas, Kidnapped by Robert Louis Stevenson, Gulliver's Travels by Jonathan Swift and Twenty Thousand Leagues Under the Sea by Jules Verne ∽ THE WAVE ∽ Gulliver
ures in Wonderland by Lewis Carroll ∽ THE MOUNTAINS ∽ Peter Pan and Wendy by J.M. Barrie ∽ THE CAVE ∽ Treasure Island by Robert Louis Stevenson and Kidnapped by Robert Louis Stevenson ∽ THE FORE
by Jacob Grimm and Wilhelm Grimm, Snow-White and Rose-Red as told by Jacob Grimm and Wilhelm Grimm, Beauty and the Beast by Jeanne-Marie Leprince de Beaumont and Rapunzel as told by Jacob Grimm and Wil
ed by Robert Bryan, Twinkle, Twinkle, Little Star by Jane Taylor, Hush-a-Bye Baby as adapted by John Newbery and Brahms' Lullaby by Johannes Brahms ∽ THE MOON ∽ Around the Moon by Jules Verne ∽ THE WO
derland by Lewis Carroll, Great Expectations by Charles Dickens, Adventures of Huckleberry Finn by Mark Twain, A Christmas Carol by Charles Dickens, Moby-Dick by Herman Melville, The Secret Garden by Frances
h Lofting, The Swiss Family Robinson by Johann David Wyss, Robinson Crusoe by Daniel Defoe, The Count of Monte Cristo by Alexandre Dumas, Kidnapped by Robert Louis Stevenson, Gulliver's Travels by Jonathan S
venty Thousand Leagues Under the Sea by Jules Verne ∽ THE HOLE ∽ Alice's Adventures in Wonderland by Lewis Carroll ∽ THE MOUNTAINS ∽ Peter Pan and Wendy by J.M. Barrie ∽ THE CAVE ∽ Treasure
nd Wilhelm Grimm, Tom Thumb as told by Richard Johnson, The Golden Bird as told by Jacob Grimm and Wilhelm Grimm, Snow-White and Rose-Red as told by Jacob Grimm and Wilhelm Grimm, Beauty and the Beas
as told by Jacob Grimm and Wilhelm Grimm ∽ THE CLOUDS ∽ Suo Gân as adapted by Robert Bryan, Twinkle, Twinkle, Little Star by Jane Taylor, Hush-a-Bye Baby as adapted by John Newbery and Brahms' Lullaby b
Dumas, The Tale of Peter Rabbit by Beatrix Potter, Alice's Adventures in Wonderland by Lewis Carroll, Great Expectations by Charles Dickens, Adventures of Huckleberry Finn by Mark Twain, A Christmas Carol by
kle by Washington Irving ∽ THE SEA ∽ The Voyages of Doctor Dolittle by Hugh Lofting, The Swiss Family Robinson by Johann David Wyss, Robinson Crusoe by Daniel Defoe, The Count of Monte Cristo by Alexan
Robinson by Johann David Wyss, The Adventures of Pinocchio by Carlo Collodi and Twenty Thousand Leagues Under the Sea by Jules Verne ∽ THE HOLE ∽ Alice's Adventures in Wonderland by Lewis Carroll ∽ TH
old by Jacob Grimm and Wilhelm Grimm, The Golden Goose as told by Jacob Grimm and Wilhelm Grimm, Tom Thumb as told by Richard Johnson, The Golden Bird as told by Jacob Grimm and Wilhelm Grimm, Snow-Wh
kenstein by Mary Shelley and Dracula by Bram Stoker ∽ THE ROPE ∽ Rapunzel as told by Jacob Grimm and Wilhelm Grimm ∽ THE CLOUDS ∽ Suo Gân as adapted by Robert Bryan, Twinkle, Twinkle, Little Star b
neth Grahame, Little Women by Louisa May Alcott, The Three Musketeers by Alexandre Dumas, The Tale of Peter Rabbit by Beatrix Potter, Alice's Adventures in Wonderland by Lewis Carroll, Great Expectations by C
g Arthur and His Knights by Sir Thomas Malory and Sir James Knowles and Rip Van Winkle by Washington Irving ∽ THE SEA ∽ The Voyages of Doctor Dolittle by Hugh Lofting, The Swiss Family Robinson by Joha
ver's Travels by Jonathan Swift, Robinson Crusoe by Daniel Defoe, The Swiss Family Robinson by Johann David Wyss, The Adventures of Pinocchio by Carlo Collodi and Twenty Thousand Leagues Under the Sea by J
∽ Little Red-Cap as told by Jacob Grimm and Wilhelm Grimm, Hansel & Gretel as told by Jacob Grimm and Wilhelm Grimm, The Golden Goose as told by Jacob Grimm and Wilhelm Grimm, Tom Thumb as told by Ric
imm ∽ THE MONSTER ∽ The Legend of Sleepy Hollow by Washington Irving, Frankenstein by Mary Shelley and Dracula by Bram Stoker ∽ THE ROPE ∽ Rapunzel as told by Jacob Grimm and Wilhelm Grimm ∽ T
he Wonderful Wizard of Oz by L. Frank Baum, The Wind in the Willows by Kenneth Grahame, Little Women by Louisa May Alcott, The Three Musketeers by Alexandre Dumas, The Tale of Peter Rabbit by Beatrix Pot
n Burnett, Heidi by Johanna Spyri, Black Beauty by Anna Sewell, The Legends of King Arthur and His Knights by Sir Thomas Malory and Sir James Knowles and Rip Van Winkle by Washington Irving ∽ THE SEA ∽ T
and Twenty Thousand Leagues Under the Sea by Jules Verne ∽ THE WAVE ∽ Gulliver's Travels by Jonathan Swift, Robinson Crusoe by Daniel Defoe, The Swiss Family Robinson by Johann David Wyss, The Adventu
d by Robert Louis Stevenson and Kidnapped by Robert Louis Stevenson ∽ THE FOREST ∽ Little Red-Cap as told by Jacob Grimm and Wilhelm Grimm, Hansel & Gretel as told by Jacob Grimm and Wilhelm Grimm, The
nne-Marie Leprince de Beaumont and Rapunzel as told by Jacob Grimm and Wilhelm Grimm ∽ THE MONSTER ∽ The Legend of Sleepy Hollow by Washington Irving, Frankenstein by Mary Shelley and Dracula by Bra
es Brahms ∽ THE MOON ∽ Around the Moon by Jules Verne ∽ THE WORLD ∽ The Wonderful Wizard of Oz by L. Frank Baum, The Wind in the Willows by Kenneth Grahame, Little Women by Louisa May Alco
arles Dickens, Moby-Dick by Herman Melville, The Secret Garden by Frances Hodgson Burnett, Heidi by Johanna Spyri, Black Beauty by Anna Sewell, The Legends of King Arthur and His Knights by Sir Thomas Malory
e Dumas, Kidnapped by Robert Louis Stevenson, Gulliver's Travels by Jonathan Swift and Twenty Thousand Leagues Under the Sea by Jules Verne ∽ THE WAVE ∽ Gulliver's Travels by Jonathan Swift, Robinson Cruso
Peter Pan and Wendy by J.M. Barrie ∽ THE CAVE ∽ Treasure Island by Robert Louis Stevenson and Kidnapped by Robert Louis Stevenson ∽ THE FOREST ∽ Little Red-Cap as told by Jacob Grimm and W

Copyright © 2016 by Oliver Jeffers and Sam Winston

All rights reserved. No part of this book may be reproduced, transmitted,
or stored in an information retrieval system in any form or by any means, graphic,
electronic, or mechanical, including photocopying, taping, and recording,
without prior written permission from the publisher.

Extract from "The Speed of Darkness" taken from *The Speed of Darkness*, New York,
Random House: 1968. Copyright © 1968 by Muriel Rukeyser. Reprinted by permission of ICM Partners.

All reasonable efforts have been made to trace the copyright holders and secure permission for the use of material used herein.
The publisher will be happy to make any necessary corrections in future printings.

First U.S. paperback edition 2021

Library of Congress Catalog Card Number 2016943940
ISBN 978-0-7636-9077-9 (hardcover)
ISBN 978-1-5362-2192-3 (paperback)

21 22 23 24 25 26 CCP 10 9 8 7 6 5 4 3 2 1

Printed in Shenzhen, Guangdong, China

This book was hand-lettered,
and the typographical landscapes
were typeset in Adobe Garamond Pro.
The illustrations were done in watercolor,
pencil, and digital collage.

Candlewick Press
99 Dover Street
Somerville, Massachusetts 02144

visit us at www.candlewick.com

CANDLEWICK PRESS

A Child of Books

Oliver JEFFERS
SAM Winston

To Lila, from Sam

To Luella, from Oliver

"The universe is made of stories, not of atoms."

Muriel Rukeyser, "The Speed of Darkness," 1968

And for Hurbinek

"Hurbinek died in the first days of March 1945, free but not redeemed.
Nothing remains of him: he bears witness through these words of mine."

Primo Levi, *If This Is a Man / The Truce,* 1947

I am a
child of books.

I come from a WORLD of STORIES

and upon my IMAGINation

...ng above the surface and throwing phosphorescent spray to great heights. Near four o'clock ...ming, the submersible picked up speed. We could barely cope with this dizzying rush, and ...lose range. **The Voyages of Doctor Dolittle** It was all so new and different: just the sky abov... ship, which was to be our house and our street, our home and our garden, for so many days t... so tiny in all this wide water – so tiny and yet so snug, sufficient, safe. I looked around me an... a deep breath. The Doctor was at the wheel steering the boat which was now leaping and plu... through the waves. (I had expected to feel seasick at first but was delighted to find that I didn't.) ...had been told off to go downstairs and prepare dinner for us. Chee-Chee was coiling up ropes in the... and laying them in neat piles. My work was fastening down the things on the deck so that nothing... roll about if the weather should grow rough when we got further from the land. Jip was up in the peak... boat with ears cocked and nose stuck out – like a statue, so still – his keen old eyes keeping a sharp look- ...floating wrecks, sand-bars, and other dangers. Each one of us had some special job to do, part of the pro... ning of a ship. Even old Polynesia was taking the sea's temperature with the Doctor's bath-thermome... on the end of a string, to make sure there were no icebergs near us. As I listened to her swearing... to herself because she couldn't read the pesky figures in the fading light, I realized that the voyage... gun in earnest and that very soon it would be night – my first night at sea! **Robinson Crusoe** A... rowed, or rather driven about a league and a half, as we reckoned it, a raging wave, mountain... that it overset the boat at once; and separating us as well from the boat as from one another, g... not time to say, "O God!" for we were all swallowed up in a moment. Nothing can describe th... sion of thought which I felt, when I sunk into the water; for though I swam very well, yet I c... not deliver myself from the waves so as to draw breath, till that wave having driven me, or ra... ried me, a vast way towards the shore, and having spent itself, went back, and left me upon... almost dry, but half dead with the water I took in. I had such presence of mind, as well as... that seeing myself nearer the mainland than I expected, I got upon my feet, and endeavour... make on towards the land as fast as I could before another wave should return and take me up... but I soon found it was impossible to avoid it; for I saw the sea come after me as high as a gr... hold my breath, and pilot myself towards the shore, if possible, my greatest concern now being that the s... and as furious as an enemy, which I had no means or strength to contend with: my business... uld carry me a great way towards the shore when it came on, might not carry me back again... when it gave back towards the sea. **The Swiss Family Robinson** Amid the roar of the thu... s I suddenly heard the cry of "Land! land!", while at the same instant the ship struck wi... rful shock, which threw everyone to the deck, and seemed to threaten her immediate... ction. Dreadful sounds betokened the breaking up of the ship, and the roaring water... in on all sides. Then the voice of the captain was heard above the tumult, shoutin... wer away the boats! We are lost!" "Lost!" I exclaimed, and the word went like a dag... my heart; but seeing my children's terror renewed, I composed myself, calling out... ully, "Take courage, my boys! We are all above water yet. There is the land not far... t us do our best to reach it. You know God helps those that help themselves!" We... t, I left them and went on deck. What was my horror when through the foam a... ay I beheld the only remaining boat leave the ship, the last of the seamen sprin... er and push off, regardless of my cries and entreaties that we might be allowed... hance of preserving their lives. My voice was drowned in the howling of the bl... d even had the crew wished it, the return of the boat was impossible. Casting... despairingly around, I became gradually aware that our position was by no m... peless, inasmuch as the stern of the ship containing our cabin was jammed be... two high rocks, and was partly raised from among the breakers which dashed... repart to pieces. As the clouds of mist and rain drove past, I could make out,... gh rents in the vaporous curtain, a line of rocky coast, and, rugged as it was,... art bounded towards it as a sign of help in the hour of need. Yet the sense of o... nely and forsaken condition weighed heavily upon me as I returned to my fa... constraining myself to say with a smile, "Courage, dear ones! Although our go... will never sail more, she is so placed that our cabin will remain above water,... morrow, if the wind and waves abate, I see no reason why we should not get a... **The Count of Monte Cristo** He saw overhead a black and tempestuous sky, ac... the wind was driving clouds that occasionally suffered a twinkling star to appe... ore him was the vast expanse of waters, sombre and terrible, whose waves foame... roared as if before the approach of a storm. Behind him, blacker than the sea, bla... an the sky, rose phantom-like the vast stone structure, whose projecting crags see... ke arms extended to seize their prey; and on the highest rock was a torch lighting t... res. He fancied that these two forms were looking at the sea; doubtless these stran... re lighthouse at Marseilles when he swam there, and was unanimously declared to be...

I Float.

Captain Hook
Dr. Dolittle

robinson crusoe
oliver twist
pinocchio
sinbad

Kidnapped ...

Gulliver's Travels It would not be proper, for some reasons, to trouble the reader with the particulars of our adventures in those seas; let it suffice to inform him, that in our passage from thence to the East Indies, we were driven by a violent storm to the north-west of Van Diemen's Land. By an observation, we found ourselves in the latitude of 30 degrees 2 minutes south. Twelve of our crew were dead by immoderate labour and ill food; the rest were in a very weak condition. On the 5th of November, which was the beginning of summer in those parts, the weather being very hazy, the seamen spied a rock within half a cable's length of the ship; but the wind was so strong, that we were driven directly upon it, and immediately split. Six of the crew, of whom I was one, having let down the boat into the sea, made a shift to get clear of the ship and the rock. We rowed, by my computation, about three leagues, till we were able to work no longer, being already spent with labour while we were in the ship. We therefore trusted ourselves to the mercy of the waves, and in about half an hour the boat was overset by a sudden flurry from the north. What became of my companions in the boat, as well as of those who escaped on the rock, or were left in the vessel, I cannot tell; but conclude they were all lost. For my own part, I swam as fortune directed me, and was pushed forward by wind and tide. I often let my legs drop, and could feel no bottom; but when I was almost gone, and able to struggle no longer, I found myself within my depth; and by this time the storm was much abated. The declivity was so small, that I walked near a mile before I got to the shore, which I conjectured was about eight o'clock in the evening. I then advanced forward near half a mile, but could not discover any sign of houses or inhabitants; at least I was in so weak a condition, that I did not observe them. I was extremely tired, and with that, and the heat of the weather, and about half a pint of brandy that I drank as I left the ship, I found myself much inclined to sleep. I lay down on the grass, which was very short and soft, where I slept sounder than ever I remember to have done in my life, and, as I reckoned, about nine hours; for when I awaked, it was just day-light. I attempted to rise, but was not able to stir: for, as I happened to lie on my back, I found my arms and legs were strongly fastened on each side to the ground; and my hair, which was long and thick, tied down in the same manner. I likewise felt several slender ligatures across my body, from my arm-pits to my thighs. I could only look upwards; the sun began to grow hot, and the light offended my eyes. I heard a confused noise about me; but in the posture I lay, could see nothing except the sky. In a little time I felt something alive moving on my left leg, which advancing gently forward over my breast, came almost up to my chin; when, bending my eyes downwards as much as I could, I perceived it to be a human creature not six inches high, with a bow and arrow in his hands, and a quiver at his back. In the mean time, I felt at least forty more. I was of the utmost astonishment, and roared so loud, that they all ran back in a fright; and some of them, as I was afterwards told, were hurt with the falls they got by leaping from my sides upon the ground.

However, they soon returned, and one of them, who ventured so far as to get a full sight of my face, lifting up his hands and eyes by way of admiration, cried out in a shrill but distinct voice, *Hekinah degul*: the others repeated the same words several times, but I then knew not what they meant. I lay all this while, as the reader may believe, in great uneasiness. **Twenty Thousand Leagues**

Under the Sea So our salvation lay totally in the hands of the mysterious helmsmen steering this submersible, and if it made a ...

I have SAILED
ACROss a SEA
of WORDS

To ask if you will
COME AWAY with ME.

SOME PEOPLE have
FORGOTTEN where
I live

SINESS

large business has rejected a
takeover proposal from another
large business which valued the first
large business for "a lot of money."
The large business said it offered "a
lot of money" and then "even more
money" but the first large business
said "that wasn't enough money"
and it wouldn't be bought out. The
first large business issued a warning
in January saying it hadn't made "a
lot of money" which prompted the
second large business to think about
buying it. "The question is, does the
large business have the money
first business?" an industry
mented.

other businesses got excited
this idea and started talking about
how much money each business was
worth. This made everyone worried
and excited, and they all waved their
arms around

ORTANT THINGS

ompany is to stop important stuff by said no one wanted of important stuff. website said – "It's sing that they have ing this thing – important after all now is to find other be important."

nnounced it would producing other bits y hoped the public ortant. "We remain oviding people with and if we can't do ll pretend they are hopefully that will ding inventor at the

also said they would stop making this particular bit of stuff as they also thought it might not be as important as they once thought it was. "What makes something really important nowadays is how much money we spend on it and if we spend vast amounts of money on it, then that obviously means it's going to be really important and we will certainly make a hoo-haa about it when we put it in the shops," said the Big Boss.

One customer did respond to this comment with "My cat is very important and that didn't cost anything!" to which the important company wrote a letter in response that said, "Dear Customer, we understand that you think your cat is very important but unfortunately you are wrong in this matter. Our leading inventor

Serious Stuff

A group of serious people passed on concerns about a serious document that has been lost by a serious organization. The serious people asked officials a long time ago to "look carefully" at this document – the serious organization initially said it had looked at this serious document last y concluded that "it wasn't that serious" and then went on to say "we have lost it." In an earlier ver looked at this document said "actually it was serious and I hope they find it." In an earlier ver story, we reported that the serious organization had started looking for the serious document. In fact, they started looking last year. So far they have looked "under chairs, rugs, and even down a sofa." Someone suggested to try looking "on the computer," but that was unsuccessful as it wasn't turned on.

In other cases like this – when someone says "this is serious" and the other says "no it isn't" – they often have to find a third person to tell them whether it's serious of the problems with people

THE FACTS

Scientists have discovered a new fact. In one test, nearly half the subjects proved the fact, it was revealed. The findings, which came from first watching people and then quizzing them, have attracted criticism from some other scientists.

The paper, published in a magazine about facts, said that their fact was true. A professor, who led the research at a university, said: rudy demonstrated

kind of thing but for do who don't – it could be rather alarming.

In fact, other researchers in the field have said the findings are overstated. The authors say this 'fact' might have been overlooked in research. Their work began with several trials involving people who were shut in a small room and tested. After 6, 12, or 15 minutes, they were asked if they had discovered this fact. On average, their answers were near the middle of a r scale.

"It
is
a long
tail, certainly,"
said Alice,
looking down
with wonder at
the Mouse's tail;
"but why do you
call it sad?" And
she kept puzzling
about it while the
Mouse was speaking,
so that her idea of the
tale was something like
this: "Fury said to a mouse,
That he met in the house, 'Let
us both go to law: I will prosecute
YOU.—Come, I'll take no
denial; We must have a trial:
For really this morning I've
nothing to do.' Said the mouse
to the cur, 'Such a trial, dear sir,
With no jury or judge, would
be wasting our breath.' 'I'll be
judge, I'll be jury,' said cunning
old Fury: 'I'll try the whole cause, and
condemn you to death.' **Alice's Adventures
in Wonderland** The rabbit-hole went strai
then dipped suddenly down, so sud   that Alice had not a
moment to think about sto   lf before she found herself falling down what seemed to be a very deep well.
Either the well was very deep, or she fell very slowly, for she had plenty of time as she went down to look about her, a

nothing of tumbling down stairs! How brave they'll all think me at home!

Down, down, down. Would the fall never come to

getting somewhere near the cent

Presently she bega

But along these WORDS
I can show you the WAY.

er what was going to happen next. First, she tried to look down and make out what

wouldn't say anything about it, even if I fell off the top of the

d? "I wonder how many miles I've fallen by this time

he earth. Let me see: that would be four thousand

n. "I wonder if I shall fall right through the earth

Down, down, down. There was nothing else to do,

but it was too dark t

was very likely true.

aloud. "I must

miles down, I

How funny

so Alice soon

WE will TRAVEL over
MOUNTAINS of MAKE-BELieve

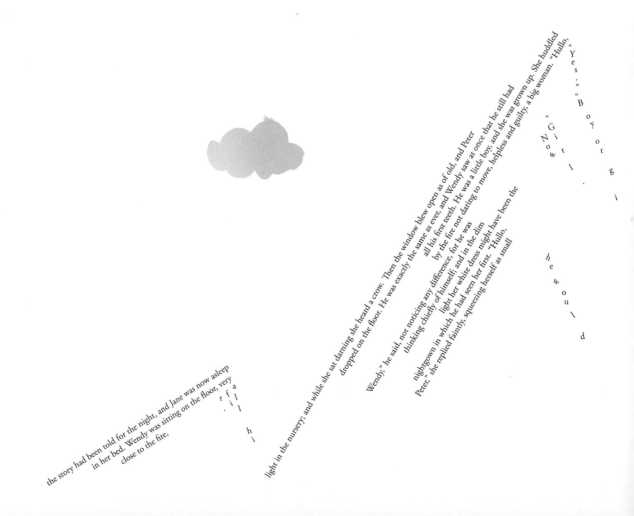

the story had been told for the night, and Jane was now asleep in her bed. Wendy was sitting on the floor, very close to the fire,

f a
r
i l
l
.
h i

light in the nursery; and while she sat darning she heard a crow. Then the window blew open as of old, and Peter dropped on the floor. He was exactly the same as ever, and Wendy saw at once that he still had all his first teeth. He was a little boy, and she was grown up. She huddled by the fire not daring to move, helpless and guilty, a big woman. "Hullo, Wendy," he said, not noticing any difference, for he was thinking chiefly of himself, and in the dim light her white dress might have been the nightgown in which he had seen her first. "Hullo, Peter," she replied faintly, squeezing herself as small

"Yes."
"Boy or girl?"
"Girl."
Now
he would

Peter Pan and Wendy

...carry her now. ...on his shoulder and gave his nose a loving bite. She whispered in his ear "You silly ass," and then, tottering to her chamber, lay down on the bed. His head almost filled the fourth wall of her little room as he knelt near her in distress. Every moment her light was growing fainter; and he knew that if it went out she would be no more. She liked his tears so much that she put out her beautiful finger and let them run over it. Her voice was so low that at first he could not make out what she said. Then he made it out. She was saying that she thought she could get well again if children believed in fairies.

Peter flung out his arms. There were no children there, and it was night-time; but he addressed all who might be dreaming of the Neverland, and who were therefore nearer to him than you think: boys and girls in their nighties; "Do you believe?" he cried. Tink sat up in bed almost briskly to listen to her fate. She fancied she heard answers in the affirmative, and then again she wasn't sure. "What do you think?" she asked Peter. "If you believe," he shouted to them, "clap your hands; don't let Tink die." Many clapped. Some didn't. A few beasts hissed. The clapping stopped suddenly; as if countless mothers had rushed to their nurseries to see what on earth was happening; but already Tink was saved. First her voice grew strong, then she popped out of bed, then she was flashing through the room more merry and impudent than ever. She never thought of thanking those who believed, but she would have liked to get at the ones who had hissed. "And now to rescue Wendy!"

The moon was riding in a cloudy heaven, when Peter rose from

with weapons and wearing little else, set out to ... his perilous

It had not been such ... He had chosen. ... hoped to fly

...now, and she ran out of the room to try to think. Peter continued to cry, and soon his sobs woke Jane. She sat up in bed, and was interested at once. "Boy," she said, "why are you crying?" Peter rose and bowed to her, and she bowed to him from the bed. "Hullo," he said. "Hullo," said Jane. "My name is Peter Pan," he explained. "Yes, I know." "I came back for my mother," he told her. "to take her to the Neverland." "Yes, I know," Jane said, "I have

...her sitting on the bed ... been waiting

DISCOVER TREASURE in the DARKNESS.

Kidnapped

I WILL BEGIN the story of my adventures with a certain morning early in the month of June, the year of grace 1751, when I took the key for the last time out of the door of my father's house. The sun began to shine upon the summit of the hills as I went down the road; and by the time I had come as far as the manse, the blackbirds were whistling in the garden lilacs, and the mist that hung around the valley in the time of the dawn was beginning to arise and die away.

Mr. Campbell, the minister of Essendean, was waiting for me by the garden gate, good man! He asked me if I had breakfasted; and hearing that I lacked for nothing, he took my hand in both of his and clapped it kindly under his arm.

"Well, Davie, lad," said he, "I will go with you as far as the ford, to set you on the way." And we began to walk forward in silence.

with soiled blue coat, his hands ragged and sc

I remember him as if it were yesterday, as he came plodding to the inn door, his sea-ch
—a tall, strong, heavy, nut-brown man, his tarry pigtail falling over the

and the sabre cut across one cheek
a dirty, livid white.

I remember him looking round the cove and whistling to himself as

It was some time before either I or the captain seemed to gather our senses;

Little **Red-Cap** It was a

happy Little Red-Cap was takin

beautiful flowers

dancing to and fro through

Once upon a time there dwelt near a large wood _**Hansel & Gretel**_

a poor

woodcutter, with his wife and

two children

a little boy called Hansel and a girl named Gretel

"What will become of us?, children, now that we

How can we feed our

discovered in a hollow under the roots a goose

plumage of pure gold

**The Golden Goose** Dummerly set to

work, and cut down

tree

when it fell

"Oh Father, cried

the

shall be in the cart

One

WE can lose
ourselves in FORESTS
of FAIRY Tales

and ESCAPE MONSTERS in HAUNTED CASTLES.

she had magnificent long hair, fine as spun gold, and when she heard the voice of the ... , she unfastened her ... tresses, wound them round one of the hooks of the window above, and then the hair fell down

Twinkle twinkle little star, how I won... above the world so hig... diamond in the sky, when the blazing sun is gone ...thing shines upon, then y... ...the night, then ...our tiny ...keep, and often through my curtains peep, for you never shut your eye, 'till the sun is in the sky, as your bright a... tiny spark, lights the tra... traveller in the dar... though I know ...little light... ...he ...winkle twinkle little star, twinkle little star, how I wonder ... a star, twinkle

Sleep my baby on my boso... round thee mother's arms are fo... warm and cosy it In her heart a mother's lo... will P.to... there shall no one naugt shall ever come to har... break thy thee rest

we will sleep

Hush-a-bye baby, on the tree top, when the wind blows the cradle will rock, when the bough breaks the cradle will fall, down will fall baby, cradle and all. Rock-a-bye baby, the cradle will rock, when the wind blows, the...

Sleep serenely, lovely baby, gently sleep. Slumber babe, wherefore art me smiling in though sleep smiling sweet! tell me smile they see?

Lullaby and good night, with roses bedight. With lilies o'er spread is baby's wee bed. Lay thee down now and rest, may thy slumber be blessed. Lullaby and good night, with lilies o'er spread is baby's Lay thee down now and rest, may thy slumber be blessed. Lullaby and good night, with lilies o'er spread is baby's wee bed. Lullaby and good night,

in clouds
of
song

could thus take observations in four different directions, having an opportunity of gazing at the firmament through the lower and the Moon through the lower and the upper lights of the Projectile. Ardan and the Captain had cor... us to operating on the bottom light. **Around the Moon** But Barbican was the first to get th... bouting: "No, my friends!" he exclaimed, in tones of decided emoti... ...rth; nor are we lying in the bottom...

and SHOUT as
LOUD
as
we like
in SPACE.

OUR HOUSE is a Home of

INVENTIon

I am a child of books. I come from a world of stories

our world we've made from stories our house is a

where ANYONE at ALL can come

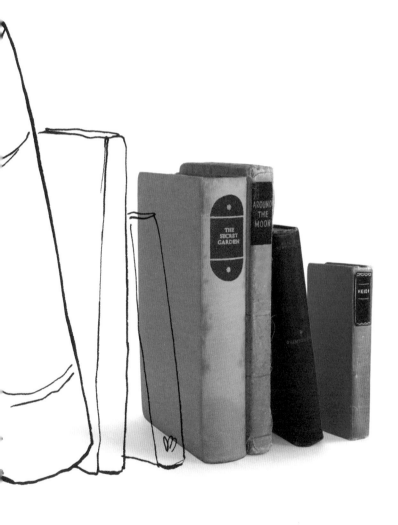

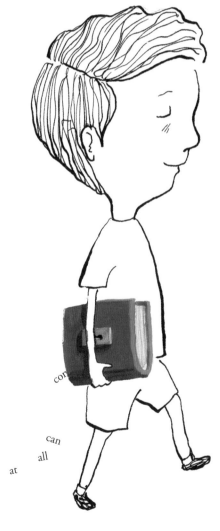

where   anyone   at   all   can   come

home   of   invention

Snow-White and Rose-Red *as told by Jacob Grimm*
by Bram Stoker ∽ THE ROPE ∽ **Rapunzel** *as told by Jacob Grimm and Wilhelm Grimm* ∽ THE CLOUDS ∽ **Suo Gân** *as adapted by Robert Bryan,* **Twinkle, Twinkle, Little Star** *by Jane Taylor,* **Hush-a-Bye Baby** *as adap*
ay Alcott, **The Three Musketeers** *by Alexandre Dumas,* **The Tale of Peter Rabbit** *by Beatrix Potter,* **Alice's Adventures in Wonderland** *by Lewis Carroll,* **Great Expectations** *by Charles Dickens,* **Adventures of Huckleberry**
Malory and Sir James Knowles and **Rip Van Winkle** *by Washington Irving* ∽ THE SEA ∽ **The Voyages of Doctor Dolittle** *by Hugh Lofting,* **The Swiss Family Robinson** *by Johann David Wyss,* **Robinson Crusoe** *by Danie*
Crusoe *by Daniel Defoe,* **The Swiss Family Robinson** *by Johann David Wyss,* **The Adventures of Pinocchio** *by Carlo Collodi* and **Twenty Thousand Leagues Under the Sea** *by Jules Verne* ∽ THE HOLE ∽ **Alice's Adv**
mm and Wilhelm Grimm, **Hansel & Gretel** *as told by Jacob Grimm and Wilhelm Grimm,* **The Golden Goose** *as told by Jacob Grimm and Wilhelm Grimm,* **Tom Thumb** *as told by Richard Johnson,* **The Golden Bird** *as told*
nd of Sleepy Hollow *by Washington Irving,* **Frankenstein** *by Mary Shelley* and **Dracula** *by Bram Stoker* ∽ THE ROPE ∽ **Rapunzel** *as told by Jacob Grimm and Wilhelm Grimm* ∽ THE CLOUDS ∽ **Suo Gân** *as adapted*
k Baum, **The Wind in the Willows** *by Kenneth Grahame,* **Little Women** *by Louisa May Alcott,* **The Three Musketeers** *by Alexandre Dumas,* **The Tale of Peter Rabbit** *by Beatrix Potter,* **Alice's Adventures in Wonderland**
auty *by Anna Sewell,* **The Legends of King Arthur and His Knights** *by Sir Thomas Malory and Sir James Knowles* and **Rip Van Winkle** *by Washington Irving* ∽ THE SEA ∽ **The Voyages of Doctor Dolittle** *by Hugh Lof*
e Sea *by Jules Verne* ∽ THE WAVE ∽ **Gulliver's Travels** *by Jonathan Swift,* **Robinson Crusoe** *by Daniel Defoe,* **The Swiss Family Robinson** *by Johann David Wyss,* **The Adventures of Pinocchio** *by Carlo Collodi* and **Tw**
ed *by Robert Louis Stevenson* ∽ THE FOREST ∽ **Little Red-Cap** *as told by Jacob Grimm and Wilhelm Grimm,* **Hansel & Gretel** *as told by Jacob Grimm and Wilhelm Grimm,* **The Golden Goose** *as told by Jacob Grimm an*
unzel *as told by Jacob Grimm and Wilhelm Grimm* ∽ THE MONSTER ∽ **The Legend of Sleepy Hollow** *by Washington Irving,* **Frankenstein** *by Mary Shelley* and **Dracula** *by Bram Stoker* ∽ THE ROPE ∽ **Rapunzel** *as t*
he Moon *by Jules Verne* ∽ THE WORLD ∽ **The Wonderful Wizard of Oz** *by L. Frank Baum,* **The Wind in the Willows** *by Kenneth Grahame,* **Little Women** *by Louisa May Alcott,* **The Three Musketeers** *by Alexandre D*
Melville, **The Secret Garden** *by Frances Hodgson Burnett,* **Heidi** *by Johanna Spyri,* **Black Beauty** *by Anna Sewell,* **The Legends of King Arthur and His Knights** *by Sir Thomas Malory and Sir James Knowles* and **Rip Van W**
venson, **Gulliver's Travels** *by Jonathan Swift* and **Twenty Thousand Leagues Under the Sea** *by Jules Verne* ∽ THE WAVE ∽ **Gulliver's Travels** *by Jonathan Swift,* **Robinson Crusoe** *by Daniel Defoe,* **The Swiss Family Rob**
J.M. Barrie ∽ THE CAVE ∽ **Treasure Island** *by Robert Louis Stevenson* and **Kidnapped** *by Robert Louis Stevenson* ∽ THE FOREST ∽ **Little Red-Cap** *as told by Jacob Grimm and Wilhelm Grimm,* **Hansel & Gretel** *as*
d Wilhelm Grimm, **Beauty and the Beast** *by Jeanne-Marie Leprince de Beaumont* and **Rapunzel** *as told by Jacob Grimm and Wilhelm Grimm* ∽ THE MONSTER ∽ **The Legend of Sleepy Hollow** *by Washington Irving,* **F**
John Newbery and **Brahms' Lullaby** *by Johannes Brahms* ∽ THE MOON ∽ **Around the Moon** *by Jules Verne* ∽ THE WORLD ∽ **The Wonderful Wizard of Oz** *by L. Frank Baum,* **The Wind in the Willows** *by Kenne*
n *by Mark Twain,* **A Christmas Carol** *by Charles Dickens,* **Moby-Dick** *by Herman Melville,* **The Secret Garden** *by Frances Hodgson Burnett,* **Heidi** *by Johanna Spyri,* **Black Beauty** *by Anna Sewell,* **The Legends of King A**
efoe, **The Count of Monte Cristo** *by Alexandre Dumas,* **Kidnapped** *by Robert Louis Stevenson,* **Gulliver's Travels** *by Jonathan Swift* and **Twenty Thousand Leagues Under the Sea** *by Jules Verne* ∽ THE WAVE ∽ **Gulliver**
es in Wonderland *by Lewis Carroll* ∽ THE MOUNTAINS ∽ **Peter Pan and Wendy** *by J.M. Barrie* ∽ THE CAVE ∽ **Treasure Island** *by Robert Louis Stevenson* and **Kidnapped** *by Robert Louis Stevenson* ∽ THE FORES
ob Grimm and Wilhelm Grimm, **Snow-White and Rose-Red** *as told by Jacob Grimm and Wilhelm Grimm,* **Beauty and the Beast** *by Jeanne-Marie Leprince de Beaumont* and **Rapunzel** *as told by Jacob Grimm and Wilhelm*
y Robert Bryan, **Twinkle, Twinkle, Little Star** *by Jane Taylor,* **Hush-a-Bye Baby** *as adapted by John Newbery* and **Brahms' Lullaby** *by Johannes Brahms* ∽ THE MOON ∽ **Around the Moon** *by Jules Verne* ∽ THE WORL
nd *by Lewis Carroll,* **Great Expectations** *by Charles Dickens,* **Adventures of Huckleberry Finn** *by Mark Twain,* **A Christmas Carol** *by Charles Dickens,* **Moby-Dick** *by Herman Melville,* **The Secret Garden** *by Frances Ho*
ing, **The Swiss Family Robinson** *by Johann David Wyss,* **Robinson Crusoe** *by Daniel Defoe,* **The Count of Monte Cristo** *by Alexandre Dumas,* **Kidnapped** *by Robert Louis Stevenson,* **Gulliver's Travels** *by Jonathan Swift a*
housand Leagues Under the Sea *by Jules Verne* ∽ THE HOLE ∽ **Alice's Adventures in Wonderland** *by Lewis Carroll* ∽ THE MOUNTAINS ∽ **Peter Pan and Wendy** *by J.M. Barrie* ∽ THE CAVE ∽ **Treasure Island**
lm Grimm, **Tom Thumb** *as told by Richard Johnson,* **The Golden Bird** *as told by Jacob Grimm and Wilhelm Grimm,* **Snow-White and Rose-Red** *as told by Jacob Grimm and Wilhelm Grimm,* **Beauty and the Beast** *by Jean*
Jacob Grimm and Wilhelm Grimm ∽ THE CLOUDS ∽ **Suo Gân** *as adapted by Robert Bryan,* **Twinkle, Twinkle, Little Star** *by Jane Taylor,* **Hush-a-Bye Baby** *as adapted by John Newbery* and **Brahms' Lullaby** *by Johanne*
he Tale of Peter Rabbit *by Beatrix Potter,* **Alice's Adventures in Wonderland** *by Lewis Carroll,* **Great Expectations** *by Charles Dickens,* **Adventures of Huckleberry Finn** *by Mark Twain,* **A Christmas Carol** *by Charles D*
gton Irving ∽ THE SEA ∽ **The Voyages of Doctor Dolittle** *by Hugh Lofting,* **The Swiss Family Robinson** *by Johann David Wyss,* **Robinson Crusoe** *by Daniel Defoe,* **The Count of Monte Cristo** *by Alexandre Dumas,* **K**
David Wyss, **The Adventures of Pinocchio** *by Carlo Collodi* and **Twenty Thousand Leagues Under the Sea** *by Jules Verne* ∽ THE HOLE ∽ **Alice's Adventures in Wonderland** *by Lewis Carroll* ∽ THE MOUNTAINS ∽
d Wilhelm Grimm, **The Golden Goose** *as told by Jacob Grimm and Wilhelm Grimm,* **Tom Thumb** *as told by Richard Johnson,* **The Golden Bird** *as told by Jacob Grimm and Wilhelm Grimm,* **Snow-White and Rose-Red** *as*
lley and **Dracula** *by Bram Stoker* ∽ THE ROPE ∽ **Rapunzel** *as told by Jacob Grimm and Wilhelm Grimm* ∽ THE CLOUDS ∽ **Suo Gân** *as adapted by Robert Bryan,* **Twinkle, Twinkle, Little Star** *by Jane Taylor,* **Hush-a-**
men *by Louisa May Alcott,* **The Three Musketeers** *by Alexandre Dumas,* **The Tale of Peter Rabbit** *by Beatrix Potter,* **Alice's Adventures in Wonderland** *by Lewis Carroll,* **Great Expectations** *by Charles Dickens,* **Adventure**
by Sir Thomas Malory and Sir James Knowles and **Rip Van Winkle** *by Washington Irving* ∽ THE SEA ∽ **The Voyages of Doctor Dolittle** *by Hugh Lofting,* **The Swiss Family Robinson** *by Johann David Wyss,* **Robinson C**
Swift, **Robinson Crusoe** *by Daniel Defoe,* **The Swiss Family Robinson** *by Johann David Wyss,* **The Adventures of Pinocchio** *by Carlo Collodi* and **Twenty Thousand Leagues Under the Sea** *by Jules Verne* ∽ THE HOLE
as told by Jacob Grimm and Wilhelm Grimm, **Hansel & Gretel** *as told by Jacob Grimm and Wilhelm Grimm,* **The Golden Goose** *as told by Jacob Grimm and Wilhelm Grimm,* **Tom Thumb** *as told by Richard Johnson,* **The G**
NSTER ∽ **The Legend of Sleepy Hollow** *by Washington Irving,* **Frankenstein** *by Mary Shelley* and **Dracula** *by Bram Stoker* ∽ THE ROPE ∽ **Rapunzel** *as told by Jacob Grimm and Wilhelm Grimm* ∽ THE CLOUDS
l Wizard of Oz *by L. Frank Baum,* **The Wind in the Willows** *by Kenneth Grahame,* **Little Women** *by Louisa May Alcott,* **The Three Musketeers** *by Alexandre Dumas,* **The Tale of Peter Rabbit** *by Beatrix Potter,* **Alice's Ac**
Johanna Spyri, **Black Beauty** *by Anna Sewell,* **The Legends of King Arthur and His Knights** *by Sir Thomas Malory and Sir James Knowles* and **Rip Van Winkle** *by Washington Irving* ∽ THE SEA ∽ **The Voyages of Doct**
l Leagues Under the Sea *by Jules Verne* ∽ THE WAVE ∽ **Gulliver's Travels** *by Jonathan Swift,* **Robinson Crusoe** *by Daniel Defoe,* **The Swiss Family Robinson** *by Johann David Wyss,* **The Adventures of Pinocchio** *by C*
enson and **Kidnapped** *by Robert Louis Stevenson* ∽ THE FOREST ∽ **Little Red-Cap** *as told by Jacob Grimm and Wilhelm Grimm,* **Hansel & Gretel** *as told by Jacob Grimm and Wilhelm Grimm,* **The Golden Goose** *as tol*
le Beaumont and **Rapunzel** *as told by Jacob Grimm and Wilhelm Grimm* ∽ THE MONSTER ∽ **The Legend of Sleepy Hollow** *by Washington Irving,* **Frankenstein** *by Mary Shelley* and **Dracula** *by Bram Stoker* ∽ THE RO
MOON ∽ **Around the Moon** *by Jules Verne* ∽ THE WORLD ∽ **The Wonderful Wizard of Oz** *by L. Frank Baum,* **The Wind in the Willows** *by Kenneth Grahame,* **Little Women** *by Louisa May Alcott,* **The Three Muske**
ck *by Herman Melville,* **The Secret Garden** *by Frances Hodgson Burnett,* **Heidi** *by Johanna Spyri,* **Black Beauty** *by Anna Sewell,* **The Legends of King Arthur and His Knights** *by Sir Thomas Malory and Sir James Knowles*
ed *by Robert Louis Stevenson,* **Gulliver's Travels** *by Jonathan Swift* and **Twenty Thousand Leagues Under the Sea** *by Jules Verne* ∽ THE WAVE ∽ **Gulliver's Travels** *by Jonathan Swift,* **Robinson Crusoe** *by Daniel Defoe,*
Pan and Wendy *by J.M. Barrie* ∽ THE CAVE ∽ **Treasure Island** *by Robert Louis Stevenson* and **Kidnapped** *by Robert Louis Stevenson* ∽ THE FOREST ∽ **Little Red-Cap** *as told by Jacob Grimm and Wilhelm Grimm,* **Ha**
Jacob Grimm and Wilhelm Grimm, **Beauty and the Beast** *by Jeanne-Marie Leprince de Beaumont* and **Rapunzel** *as told by Jacob Grimm and Wilhelm Grimm* ∽ THE MONSTER ∽ **The Legend of Sleepy Hollow** *by Wash*
Bye Baby *as adapted by John Newbery* and **Brahms' Lullaby** *by Johannes Brahms* ∽ THE MOON ∽ **Around the Moon** *by Jules Verne* ∽ THE WORLD ∽ **The Wonderful Wizard of Oz** *by L. Frank Baum,* **The Wind in th**
es of Huckleberry Finn *by Mark Twain,* **A Christmas Carol** *by Charles Dickens,* **Moby-Dick** *by Herman Melville,* **The Secret Garden** *by Frances Hodgson Burnett,* **Heidi** *by Johanna Spyri,* **Black Beauty** *by Anna Sewell,* **Th**
Crusoe *by Daniel Defoe,* **The Count of Monte Cristo** *by Alexandre Dumas,* **Kidnapped** *by Robert Louis Stevenson,* **Gulliver's Travels** *by Jonathan Swift* and **Twenty Thousand Leagues Under the Sea** *by Jules Verne* ∽ TH
Alice's Adventures in Wonderland *by Lewis Carroll* ∽ THE MOUNTAINS ∽ **Peter Pan and Wendy** *by J.M. Barrie* ∽ THE CAVE ∽ **Treasure Island** *by Robert Louis Stevenson* and **Kidnapped** *by Robert Louis Stevenson*
Bird *as told by Jacob Grimm and Wilhelm Grimm,* **Snow-White and Rose-Red** *as told by Jacob Grimm and Wilhelm Grimm,* **Beauty and the Beast** *by Jeanne-Marie Leprince de Beaumont* and **Rapunzel** *as told by Jacob Grim*
as adapted by Robert Bryan, **Twinkle, Twinkle, Little Star** *by Jane Taylor,* **Hush-a-Bye Baby** *as adapted by John Newbery* and **Brahms' Lullaby** *by Johannes Brahms* ∽ THE MOON ∽ **Around the Moon** *by Jules Verne*
es in Wonderland *by Lewis Carroll,* **Great Expectations** *by Charles Dickens,* **Adventures of Huckleberry Finn** *by Mark Twain,* **A Christmas Carol** *by Charles Dickens,* **Moby-Dick** *by Herman Melville,* **The Secret Garden**
olittle *by Hugh Lofting,* **The Swiss Family Robinson** *by Johann David Wyss,* **Robinson Crusoe** *by Daniel Defoe,* **The Count of Monte Cristo** *by Alexandre Dumas,* **Kidnapped** *by Robert Louis Stevenson,* **Gulliver's Travels**
Collodi and **Twenty Thousand Leagues Under the Sea** *by Jules Verne* ∽ THE HOLE ∽ **Alice's Adventures in Wonderland** *by Lewis Carroll* ∽ THE MOUNTAINS ∽ **Peter Pan and Wendy** *by J.M. Barrie* ∽ THE CAVE
ob Grimm and Wilhelm Grimm, **Tom Thumb** *as told by Richard Johnson,* **The Golden Bird** *as told by Jacob Grimm and Wilhelm Grimm,* **Snow-White and Rose-Red** *as told by Jacob Grimm and Wilhelm Grimm,* **Beauty an**
Rapunzel *as told by Jacob Grimm and Wilhelm Grimm* ∽ THE CLOUDS ∽ **Suo Gân** *as adapted by Robert Bryan,* **Twinkle, Twinkle, Little Star** *by Jane Taylor,* **Hush-a-Bye Baby** *as adapted by John Newbery* and **Brahms'**
rs by Alexandre Dumas, **The Tale of Peter Rabbit** *by Beatrix Potter,* **Alice's Adventures in Wonderland** *by Lewis Carroll,* **Great Expectations** *by Charles Dickens,* **Adventures of Huckleberry Finn** *by Mark Twain,* **A Chris**
nd Rip Van Winkle *by Washington Irving* ∽ THE SEA ∽ **The Voyages of Doctor Dolittle** *by Hugh Lofting,* **The Swiss Family Robinson** *by Johann David Wyss,* **Robinson Crusoe** *by Daniel Defoe,* **The Count of Monte**
Family Robinson *by Johann David Wyss,* **The Adventures of Pinocchio** *by Carlo Collodi* and **Twenty Thousand Leagues Under the Sea** *by Jules Verne* ∽ THE HOLE ∽ **Alice's Adventures in Wonderland** *by Lewis C*

Beauty and the Beast *by Jeanne-Marie Leprince de Beaumont* and Rapunzel *as told by Jacob Grimm and Wilhelm Grimm* and **Brahms' Lullaby** *by Johannes Brahms* ∽ THE MOON ∽ **Around the Moon** *by Jules Verne* ∽ THE WORLD ∽ **The Wonderful Wizard of Oz** *by L. Frank Baum*, **The Wind in the Willows** *by Kenneth Grahame*, Li

n, **A Christmas Carol** *by Charles Dickens*, **Moby-Dick** *by Herman Melville*, **The Secret Garden** *by Frances Hodgson Burnett*, **Heidi** *by Johanna Spyri*, **Black Beauty** *by Anna Sewell*, **The Legends of King Arthur and His K**

of Monte Cristo *by Alexandre Dumas*, **Kidnapped** *by Robert Louis Stevenson*, **Gulliver's Travels** *by Jonathan Swift* and **Twenty Thousand Leagues Under the Sea** *by Jules Verne* ∽ THE WAVE ∽ **Gulliver's Travels** *by Jona*

nd *by Lewis Carroll* ∽ THE MOUNTAINS ∽ **Peter Pan and Wendy** *by J.M. Barrie* ∽ THE CAVE ∽ **Treasure Island** *by Robert Louis Stevenson* and **Kidnapped** *by Robert Louis Stevenson* ∽ THE FOREST ∽ **Little Red**

Wilhelm Grimm, **Snow-White and Rose-Red** *as told by Jacob Grimm and Wilhelm Grimm*, **Beauty and the Beast** *by Jeanne-Marie Leprince de Beaumont* and **Rapunzel** *as told by Jacob Grimm and Wilhelm Grimm* ∽ THE

nkle, Twinkle, Little Star *by Jane Taylor*, **Hush-a-Bye Baby** *as adapted by John Newbery* and **Brahms' Lullaby** *by Johannes Brahms* ∽ THE MOON ∽ **Around the Moon** *by Jules Verne* ∽ THE WORLD ∽ **The Wonder**

eat Expectations *by Charles Dickens*, **Adventures of Huckleberry Finn** *by Mark Twain*, **A Christmas Carol** *by Charles Dickens*, **Moby-Dick** *by Herman Melville*, **The Secret Garden** *by Frances Hodgson Burnett*, **Heidi** *by*

ily Robinson *by Johann David Wyss*, **Robinson Crusoe** *by Daniel Defoe*, **The Count of Monte Cristo** *by Alexandre Dumas*, **Kidnapped** *by Robert Louis Stevenson*, **Gulliver's Travels** *by Jonathan Swift* and **Twenty Thousar**

ues Under the Sea *by Jules Verne* ∽ THE HOLE ∽ **Alice's Adventures in Wonderland** *by Lewis Carroll* ∽ THE MOUNTAINS ∽ **Peter Pan and Wendy** *by J.M. Barrie* ∽ THE CAVE ∽ **Treasure Island** *by Robert Loui*

om Thumb *as told by Richard Johnson*, **The Golden Bird** *as told by Jacob Grimm and Wilhelm Grimm*, **Snow-White and Rose-Red** *as told by Jacob Grimm and Wilhelm Grimm*, **Beauty and the Beast** *by Jeanne-Marie Lep*

nd Wilhelm Grimm ∽ THE CLOUDS ∽ **Suo Gân** *as adapted by Robert Bryan*, **Twinkle, Twinkle, Little Star** *by Jane Taylor*, **Hush-a-Bye Baby** *as adapted by John Newbery* and **Brahms' Lullaby** *by Johannes Brahms* ∽ TH

eter Rabbit *by Beatrix Potter*, **Alice's Adventures in Wonderland** *by Lewis Carroll*, **Great Expectations** *by Charles Dickens*, **Adventures of Huckleberry Finn** *by Mark Twain*, **A Christmas Carol** *by Charles Dickens*, **Moby**

Irving ∽ THE SEA ∽ **The Voyages of Doctor Dolittle** *by Hugh Lofting*, **The Swiss Family Robinson** *by Johann David Wyss*, **Robinson Crusoe** *by Daniel Defoe*, **The Count of Monte Cristo** *by Alexandre Dumas*, Kidn

vid Wyss, **The Adventures of Pinocchio** *by Carlo Collodi* and **Twenty Thousand Leagues Under the Sea** *by Jules Verne* ∽ THE HOLE ∽ **Alice's Adventures in Wonderland** *by Lewis Carroll* ∽ THE MOUNTAINS ∽ P

and Wilhelm Grimm, **The Golden Goose** *as told by Jacob Grimm and Wilhelm Grimm*, **Tom Thumb** *as told by Richard Johnson*, **The Golden Bird** *as told by Jacob Grimm and Wilhelm Grimm*, **Snow-White and Rose-Red**

y Shelley and **Dracula** *by Bram Stoker* ∽ THE ROPE ∽ **Rapunzel** *as told by Jacob Grimm and Wilhelm Grimm* ∽ THE CLOUDS ∽ **Suo Gân** *as adapted by Robert Bryan*, **Twinkle, Twinkle, Little Star** *by Jane Taylor*, Hu

Women *by Louisa May Alcott*, **The Three Musketeers** *by Alexandre Dumas*, **The Tale of Peter Rabbit** *by Beatrix Potter*, **Alice's Adventures in Wonderland** *by Lewis Carroll*, **Great Expectations** *by Charles Dickens*, **Adventu**

hts *by Sir Thomas Malory and Sir James Knowles* and **Rip Van Winkle** *by Washington Irving* ∽ THE SEA ∽ **The Voyages of Doctor Dolittle** *by Hugh Lofting*, **The Swiss Family Robinson** *by Johann David Wyss*, Robinso

n Swift, **Robinson Crusoe** *by Daniel Defoe*, **The Swiss Family Robinson** *by Johann David Wyss*, **The Adventures of Pinocchio** *by Carlo Collodi* and **Twenty Thousand Leagues Under the Sea** *by Jules Verne* ∽ THE HOI

p *as told by Jacob Grimm and Wilhelm Grimm*, **Hansel & Gretel** *as told by Jacob Grimm and Wilhelm Grimm*, **The Golden Goose** *as told by Jacob Grimm and Wilhelm Grimm*, **Tom Thumb** *as told by Richard Johnson*, The

NSTER ∽ **The Legend of Sleepy Hollow** *by Washington Irving*, **Frankenstein** *by Mary Shelley* and **Dracula** *by Bram Stoker* ∽ THE ROPE ∽ **Rapunzel** *as told by Jacob Grimm and Wilhelm Grimm* ∽ THE CLOUDS ∽

l Wizard of Oz *by L. Frank Baum*, **The Wind in the Willows** *by Kenneth Grahame*, **Little Women** *by Louisa May Alcott*, **The Three Musketeers** *by Alexandre Dumas*, **The Tale of Peter Rabbit** *by Beatrix Potter*, **Alice's Ad**

by Johanna Spyri, **Black Beauty** *by Anna Sewell*, **The Legends of King Arthur and His Knights** *by Sir Thomas Malory and Sir James Knowles* and **Rip Van Winkle** *by Washington Irving* ∽ THE SEA ∽ **The Voyages of D**

nd Leagues Under the Sea *by Jules Verne* ∽ THE WAVE ∽ **Gulliver's Travels** *by Jonathan Swift*, **Robinson Crusoe** *by Daniel Defoe*, **The Swiss Family Robinson** *by Johann David Wyss*, **The Adventures of Pinocchio** *by*

enson and **Kidnapped** *by Robert Louis Stevenson* ∽ THE FOREST ∽ **Little Red-Cap** *as told by Jacob Grimm and Wilhelm Grimm*, **Hansel & Gretel** *as told by Jacob Grimm and Wilhelm Grimm*, **The Golden Goose** *as told*

Beaumont and **Rapunzel** *as told by Jacob Grimm and Wilhelm Grimm* ∽ THE MONSTER ∽ **The Legend of Sleepy Hollow** *by Washington Irving*, **Frankenstein** *by Mary Shelley* and **Dracula** *by Bram Stoker* ∽ THE RO

OON ∽ **Around the Moon** *by Jules Verne* ∽ THE WORLD ∽ **The Wonderful Wizard of Oz** *by L. Frank Baum*, **The Wind in the Willows** *by Kenneth Grahame*, **Little Women** *by Louisa May Alcott*, **The Three Muskete**

by Herman Melville, **The Secret Garden** *by Frances Hodgson Burnett*, **Heidi** *by Johanna Spyri*, **Black Beauty** *by Anna Sewell*, **The Legends of King Arthur and His Knights** *by Sir Thomas Malory and Sir James Knowles* and

Louis Stevenson, **Gulliver's Travels** *by Jonathan Swift* and **Twenty Thousand Leagues Under the Sea** *by Jules Verne* ∽ THE WAVE ∽ **Gulliver's Travels** *by Jonathan Swift*, **Robinson Crusoe** *by Daniel Defoe*, **The Swiss Fa**

endy *by J.M. Barrie* ∽ THE CAVE ∽ **Treasure Island** *by Robert Louis Stevenson* and **Kidnapped** *by Robert Louis Stevenson* ∽ THE FOREST ∽ **Little Red-Cap** *as told by Jacob Grimm and Wilhelm Grimm*, **Hansel & Gre**

n and Wilhelm Grimm, **Beauty and the Beast** *by Jeanne-Marie Leprince de Beaumont* and **Rapunzel** *as told by Jacob Grimm and Wilhelm Grimm* ∽ THE MONSTER ∽ **The Legend of Sleepy Hollow** *by Washington Irving*

d John Newbery and **Brahms' Lullaby** *by Johannes Brahms* ∽ THE MOON ∽ **Around the Moon** *by Jules Verne* ∽ THE WORLD ∽ **The Wonderful Wizard of Oz** *by L. Frank Baum*, **The Wind in the Willows** *by Ken*

inn *by Mark Twain*, **A Christmas Carol** *by Charles Dickens*, **Moby-Dick** *by Herman Melville*, **The Secret Garden** *by Frances Hodgson Burnett*, **Heidi** *by Johanna Spyri*, **Black Beauty** *by Anna Sewell*, **The Legends of King A**

o, **The Count of Monte Cristo** *by Alexandre Dumas*, **Kidnapped** *by Robert Louis Stevenson*, **Gulliver's Travels** *by Jonathan Swift* and **Twenty Thousand Leagues Under the Sea** *by Jules Verne* ∽ THE WAVE ∽ **Gulliver's**

res in Wonderland *by Lewis Carroll* ∽ THE MOUNTAINS ∽ **Peter Pan and Wendy** *by J.M. Barrie* ∽ THE CAVE ∽ **Treasure Island** *by Robert Louis Stevenson* and **Kidnapped** *by Robert Louis Stevenson* ∽ THE FORES

y Jacob Grimm and Wilhelm Grimm, **Snow-White and Rose-Red** *as told by Jacob Grimm and Wilhelm Grimm*, **Beauty and the Beast** *by Jeanne-Marie Leprince de Beaumont* and **Rapunzel** *as told by Jacob Grimm and Wilh*

d *by Robert Bryan*, **Twinkle, Twinkle, Little Star** *by Jane Taylor*, **Hush-a-Bye Baby** *as adapted by John Newbery* and **Brahms' Lullaby** *by Johannes Brahms* ∽ THE MOON ∽ **Around the Moon** *by Jules Verne* ∽ THE WOR

erland *by Lewis Carroll*, **Great Expectations** *by Charles Dickens*, **Adventures of Huckleberry Finn** *by Mark Twain*, **A Christmas Carol** *by Charles Dickens*, **Moby-Dick** *by Herman Melville*, **The Secret Garden** *by Frances A*

Lofting, **The Swiss Family Robinson** *by Johann David Wyss*, **Robinson Crusoe** *by Daniel Defoe*, **The Count of Monte Cristo** *by Alexandre Dumas*, **Kidnapped** *by Robert Louis Stevenson*, **Gulliver's Travels** *by Jonathan Su*

enty Thousand Leagues Under the Sea *by Jules Verne* ∽ THE HOLE ∽ **Alice's Adventures in Wonderland** *by Lewis Carroll* ∽ THE MOUNTAINS ∽ **Peter Pan and Wendy** *by J.M. Barrie* ∽ THE CAVE ∽ **Treasure Is**

d Wilhelm Grimm, **Tom Thumb** *as told by Richard Johnson*, **The Golden Bird** *as told by Jacob Grimm and Wilhelm Grimm*, **Snow-White and Rose-Red** *as told by Jacob Grimm and Wilhelm Grimm*, **Beauty and the Beast** a

told by Jacob Grimm and Wilhelm Grimm ∽ THE CLOUDS ∽ **Suo Gân** *as adapted by Robert Bryan*, **Twinkle, Twinkle, Little Star** *by Jane Taylor*, **Hush-a-Bye Baby** *as adapted by John Newbery* and **Brahms' Lullaby** *by*

Dumas, **The Tale of Peter Rabbit** *by Beatrix Potter*, **Alice's Adventures in Wonderland** *by Lewis Carroll*, **Great Expectations** *by Charles Dickens*, **Adventures of Huckleberry Finn** *by Mark Twain*, **A Christmas Carol** *by C*

le *by Washington Irving* ∽ THE SEA ∽ **The Voyages of Doctor Dolittle** *by Hugh Lofting*, **The Swiss Family Robinson** *by Johann David Wyss*, **Robinson Crusoe** *by Daniel Defoe*, **The Count of Monte Cristo** *by Alexandr*

obinson *by Johann David Wyss*, **The Adventures of Pinocchio** *by Carlo Collodi* and **Twenty Thousand Leagues Under the Sea** *by Jules Verne* ∽ THE HOLE ∽ **Alice's Adventures in Wonderland** *by Lewis Carroll* ∽ TH

d by Jacob Grimm and Wilhelm Grimm, **The Golden Goose** *as told by Jacob Grimm and Wilhelm Grimm*, **Tom Thumb** *as told by Richard Johnson*, **The Golden Bird** *as told by Jacob Grimm and Wilhelm Grimm*, **Snow-Whi**

kenstein *by Mary Shelley* and **Dracula** *by Bram Stoker* ∽ THE ROPE ∽ **Rapunzel** *as told by Jacob Grimm and Wilhelm Grimm* ∽ THE CLOUDS ∽ **Suo Gân** *as adapted by Robert Bryan*, **Twinkle, Twinkle, Little Star** *by*

neth Grahame, **Little Women** *by Louisa May Alcott*, **The Three Musketeers** *by Alexandre Dumas*, **The Tale of Peter Rabbit** *by Beatrix Potter*, **Alice's Adventures in Wonderland** *by Lewis Carroll*, **Great Expectations** *by Cha*

g Arthur and His Knights *by Sir Thomas Malory and Sir James Knowles* and **Rip Van Winkle** *by Washington Irving* ∽ THE SEA ∽ **The Voyages of Doctor Dolittle** *by Hugh Lofting*, **The Swiss Family Robinson** *by Johan*

er's Travels *by Jonathan Swift*, **Robinson Crusoe** *by Daniel Defoe*, **The Swiss Family Robinson** *by Johann David Wyss*, **The Adventures of Pinocchio** *by Carlo Collodi* and **Twenty Thousand Leagues Under the Sea** *by Ju*

∽ Little Red-Cap *as told by Jacob Grimm and Wilhelm Grimm*, **Hansel & Gretel** *as told by Jacob Grimm and Wilhelm Grimm*, **The Golden Goose** *as told by Jacob Grimm and Wilhelm Grimm*, **Tom Thumb** *as told by Rich*

mm ∽ THE MONSTER ∽ **The Legend of Sleepy Hollow** *by Washington Irving*, **Frankenstein** *by Mary Shelley* and **Dracula** *by Bram Stoker* ∽ THE ROPE ∽ **Rapunzel** *as told by Jacob Grimm and Wilhelm Grimm* ∽ TH

he Wonderful Wizard of Oz *by L. Frank Baum*, **The Wind in the Willows** *by Kenneth Grahame*, **Little Women** *by Louisa May Alcott*, **The Three Musketeers** *by Alexandre Dumas*, **The Tale of Peter Rabbit** *by Beatrix Potte*

a Burnett, **Heidi** *by Johanna Spyri*, **Black Beauty** *by Anna Sewell*, **The Legends of King Arthur and His Knights** *by Sir Thomas Malory and Sir James Knowles* and **Rip Van Winkle** *by Washington Irving* ∽ THE SEA ∽ Th

and Twenty Thousand Leagues Under the Sea *by Jules Verne* ∽ THE WAVE ∽ **Gulliver's Travels** *by Jonathan Swift*, **Robinson Crusoe** *by Daniel Defoe*, **The Swiss Family Robinson** *by Johann David Wyss*, **The Adventur**

by Robert Louis Stevenson and **Kidnapped** *by Robert Louis Stevenson* ∽ THE FOREST ∽ **Little Red-Cap** *as told by Jacob Grimm and Wilhelm Grimm*, **Hansel & Gretel** *as told by Jacob Grimm and Wilhelm Grimm*, **The C**

ine-Marie Leprince de Beaumont and **Rapunzel** *as told by Jacob Grimm and Wilhelm Grimm* ∽ THE MONSTER ∽ **The Legend of Sleepy Hollow** *by Washington Irving*, **Frankenstein** *by Mary Shelley* and **Dracula** *by Bra*

Brahms ∽ THE MOON ∽ **Around the Moon** *by Jules Verne* ∽ THE WORLD ∽ **The Wonderful Wizard of Oz** *by L. Frank Baum*, **The Wind in the Willows** *by Kenneth Grahame*, **Little Women** *by Louisa May Alcott*,

rles Dickens, **Moby-Dick** *by Herman Melville*, **The Secret Garden** *by Frances Hodgson Burnett*, **Heidi** *by Johanna Spyri*, **Black Beauty** *by Anna Sewell*, **The Legends of King Arthur and His Knights** *by Sir Thomas Malory a*

Dumas, **Kidnapped** *by Robert Louis Stevenson*, **Gulliver's Travels** *by Jonathan Swift* and **Twenty Thousand Leagues Under the Sea** *by Jules Verne* ∽ THE WAVE ∽ **Gulliver's Travels** *by Jonathan Swift*, **Robinson Crusoe** *by*

TAINS ∽ **Peter Pan and Wendy** *by J.M. Barrie* ∽ THE CAVE ∽ **Treasure Island** *by Robert Louis Stevenson* and **Kidnapped** *by Robert Louis Stevenson* ∽ THE FOREST ∽ **Little Red-Cap** *as told by Jacob Grimm and W*

Oliver Jeffers is an artist and storyteller whose work takes many forms. Known for his distinctive illustrations and handwritten type, he is also a figurative painter and installation artist. His much-loved picture books, including *Here We Are*, *Lost and Found*, which inspired the BAFTA-winning short film, and the *New York Times* bestseller *The Day the Crayons Quit* and its sequel, written by Drew Daywalt, have received numerous awards and have been translated into more than thirty languages. Originally from Northern Ireland, Oliver Jeffers is now based in Brooklyn, New York.

Sam Winston is a fine artist who has exhibited his work in museums and galleries all over the world. The Tate Britain, the British Library, the Library of Congress in Washington, D.C., the MoMA, and Stanford University, amongst many others, hold his artist's books in their permanent collections. Sam lives and works in London. Discover more of his work at www.samwinston.com and on social media @samwinston_.